Funeral

**Faber
Stories**

John McGahern was born in Dublin in 1934 and brought up in the West of Ireland. He was a graduate of University College, Dublin. He worked as a primary school teacher and held various academic posts at universities in Britain, Ireland and America. The author of six highly acclaimed novels and four collections of short stories, he was the recipient of numerous awards and honours, including a Society of Authors Travelling Scholarship, the American-Irish Award and the Prix Etrangère Ecureuil, and was made a Chevalier de l'Ordre des Arts et des Lettres. *Amongst Women*, which won both the GPA and the *Irish Times* Award, was shortlisted for the Booker Prize and made into a four-part BBC television series. His last book, *Memoir*, was published in 2005. He died in 2006.

John
McGahern

The
Country
Funeral

Faber
Stories

ff

First published in this single edition in 2019
by Faber & Faber Limited
Bloomsbury House
74–77 Great Russell Street
London WC1B 3DA
First published in *Collected Stories* in 1992

Typeset by Faber & Faber Limited
Printed and bound by CPI Group (UK) Ltd, Croydon, CR0 4YY

A CIP record for this book
is available from the British Library

ISBN 978–0–571–35184–8

10 9 8 7 6 5 4 3 2 1

After Fonsie Ryan called his brother he sat in his wheelchair and waited with growing impatience for him to appear on the small stairs and then, as soon as Philly came down and sat at the table, Fonsie moved his wheelchair to the far wall to wait for him to finish. This silent pressure exasperated Philly as he ate.

'Did Mother get up yet?' he asked abruptly.

'She didn't feel like getting up. She went back to sleep after I brought her tea.'

Philly let his level stare rest on his brother but all Fonsie did was to move his wheelchair a few inches out from the wall and then, in the same leaning rocking movement, let it the same few inches back, his huge hands all the time gripping the wheels. With his large head and trunk, he sometimes looked like a circus dwarf. The legless trousers were sewn up below the hips.

Slowly and deliberately Philly buttered the toast, picked at the rashers and egg and sausages, took slow sips from his cup, but his nature was not hard. As quickly as he had grown angry he softened towards his brother.

'Would you be interested in pushing down to Mulligan's after a while for a pint?'

'I have the shopping to do.'

'Don't let me hold you up, then,' Philly responded sharply to the rebuff. 'I'll be well able to let myself out.'

'There's no hurry. I'll wait and wash up. It's nice to come back to a clean house.'

'I can wash these things up. I do it all the time in Saudi Arabia.'

'You're on your holidays now,' Fonsie said. 'I'm in no rush but it's too early in the day for me to drink.'

Three weeks before, Philly had come home in a fever of excitement from the oil fields. He always came home in that high state of fever and it lasted for a few days in the distribution of the presents he always brought home, especially to his mother; his delight looking at her sparse filigreed hair bent over the rug he had brought her, the bright tassels resting on her fingers; the meetings with old school friends, the meetings with neighbours, the buying of rounds and rounds of drinks; his own fever for company after the months at the oil wells and delight in the rounds of celebration blinding him to the poor fact that it is not generally light but shadow that we cast; and now all that fever had subsided to leave him alone and companionless in just another morning as he left the house without further word to Fonsie and with nothing better to do than walk to Mulligan's.

Because of the good weather, many of the terrace doors were open and people sat in the doorways, their feet out on the pavement. A young blonde woman was painting her toenails red in the shadow of a pram in a doorway at the end of the terrace, and she did not look up as he passed. Increasingly people had their own lives here and his homecoming broke the monotony for a few days, and then he did not belong.

As soon as the barman in Mulligan's had pulled his pint he offered Philly the newspaper spread out on the counter that he had been reading.

'Don't you want it yourself?' Philly asked out of a sense of politeness.

'I must have been through it at least twice. I've the complete arse read out of it since the morning.'

There were three other drinkers scattered about the bar nursing their pints at tables.

There's never anything in those newspapers,' one of the drinkers said.

'Still, you always think you'll come on something,' the barman responded hopefully.

'That's how they get your money,' the drinker said.

Feet passed the open doorway. When it was empty the concrete gave back its own grey dull light. Philly turned the pages slowly and sipped at the pint. The waiting silence of the bar became too close an echo of the emptiness he felt all around his life. As he sipped and turned the pages he resolved to drink no more. The day would be too hard to get through if he had more. He'd go back to the house and tell his mother he was returning early to the oil fields. There were other places he could kill time in. London and Naples were on the way to Bahrain.

'He made a great splash when he came home first,' one of the drinkers said to the empty bar as soon as Philly left. 'He bought rings round him. Now the brother in the wheelchair isn't with him any more.'

'Too much. Too much,' a second drinker added forcefully though it wasn't clear at all to what he referred.

'It must be bad when that brother throws in the towel, because he's a tank for drink. You'd think there was no bottom in that wheelchair.'

The barman stared in silent disapproval at his three customers. There were few things he disliked more than this 'behind-backs' criticism of a customer as soon as he left. He opened the newspaper loudly, staring pointedly out at the three drinkers until they were silent, and then bent his head to travel slowly through the pages again.

'I heard a good one the other day,' one of the drinkers cackled rebelliously. 'The only chance of travel that ever comes to the poor is when they get sick. They go from one state to the other state and back again to base if they're lucky.'

The other two thought this hilarious and one pounded the table with his glass in appreciation. Then they looked towards the barman for approval but he just raised his eyes to stare absently out on the grey strip of concrete until the little insurrection died and he was able to continue travelling through the newspaper again.

Philly came slowly back up the street. The blonde had finished painting her toenails – a loud vermilion – and she leaned the back of her head against a door jamb, her eyes closing as she gave her face and throat completely to the sun. The hooded pram above her outstretched legs was silent. Away, behind the area railings, old men wearing berets were playing bowls, a miniature French flag flying on the railings.

Philly expected to enter an empty room but as soon as he put his key in the door he heard the raised voices. He held the key still. His mother was downstairs. She and Fonsie were arguing. With a welcome little rush of expectancy, he turned the key. The two were so engaged with one another that they did not notice him enter. His mother was in her blue dressing gown. She stood remarkably erect.

'What's going on?' They were so involved with one another that they looked towards him as if he were a burglar.

'Your Uncle Peter died last night, in Gloria. The Cullens just phoned,' his mother said, and it was Philly's turn to look at his mother and brother as if he couldn't quite grasp why they were in the room.

'You'll all have to go,' his mother said.

'I don't see why we should have to go. We haven't seen the man in twenty years. He never even liked us,' Fonsie said heatedly, turning the wheelchair to face Philly.

'Of course we'll go. We are all he has now. It wouldn't look right if we didn't go down.' Philly would have grasped at any diversion, but the pictures of Gloria Bog that flooded his mind shut out the day and the room with amazing brightness and calm.

'That doesn't mean I have to go,' Fonsie said.

'Of course you have to go. He was your uncle as well as mine,' Philly said.

'If nobody went to poor Peter's funeral, God rest him, we'd be the talk of the countryside for years,' their mother said. 'If I know nothing else in the world I know what they're like down there.'

'Anyhow, there's no way I can go in this.' Fonsie gestured contemptuously to his wheelchair.

'That's no problem. I'll hire a Mercedes. With a jalopy like that you wouldn't think of coming yourself, Mother?' Philly asked suddenly with the humour and malice of deep knowledge, and the silence that met the suggestion was as great as if some gross obscenity had been uttered.

'I'd look a nice speck in Gloria when I haven't been out of my own house in years. There wouldn't be much point in going to poor Peter's funeral, God rest him, and turning up at my own,' she said in a voice in which a sudden frailty only served to point up the different shades of its steel.

'He never even liked us. There were times I felt if he got a chance he'd throw me into a bog hole the way he drowned the black whippet that started eating the eggs,' Philly said.

'He's gone now,' the mother said. 'He stood to us when he was needed. It made no difference whether he liked us or not.'

'How will you manage on your own?' Fonsie asked as if he had accepted he'd have to go.

'Won't Mrs O'Brien next door look in if you ask her and can't I call her myself on the phone? It'll be good for you to get out of the city for a change. None of the rest can be trusted to bring me back a word of anything that goes on,' she flattered.

'Was John told yet?' Philly interrupted, asking about their eldest brother.

'No. There'd be no use ringing him at home now. You'd have to ring him at the school,' their mother said.

The school's number was written in a notebook. Philly had to wait a long time on the phone after he explained the urgency of the call while the school secretary got John from the classroom.

'John won't take time off school to go to any funeral,' Fonsie said confidently as they waited.

To Fonsie's final disgust John agreed to go to the

funeral at once. He'd be waiting for them at whatever time they thought they'd be ready to travel.

Philly hired the Mercedes. The wheelchair folded easily into its cavern-like boot. 'You'll all be careful,' their mother counselled as she kissed them goodbye. 'Everything you do down there will be watched and gone over. I'll be following poor Peter in my mind until you rest him with Father and Mother in Killeelan.'

John was waiting for them outside his front door, a brown hat in his hand, a gabardine raincoat folded on his arm, when the Mercedes pulled up at the low double gate. Before Philly had time to touch the horn John raised the hat and hurried down the concrete path. On both sides of the path the postage-stamp lawns showed the silver tracks of a mower, and roses were stacked and tied along the earthen borders.

'The wife doesn't seem to appear at all these days?' Philly asked, the vibrations of the engine shaking the car as they waited while John closed the gate.

'Herself and Mother never pulled,' Fonsie offered.

There was dull peace between the two brothers now. Fonsie knew he was more or less in Philly's hands for the next two days. He did not like it but the stupid death had moved the next two days out of his control.

'What's she like now?'

'I suppose she's much like the rest of us. She was always nippy.'

'I'm sorry for keeping you,' John said as he got into the back of the car.

'You didn't keep us at all,' Philly answered.

'It's great to get a sudden break like this. You can't imagine what it is to get out of the school and city for two or three whole days,' John said before he settled and was silent. The big Mercedes grew silent as it gathered speed through Fairview and the North Strand, crossing the Liffey at the Custom House, and turned into the one-way flow of traffic out along the south bank of the river. Not until they got past Leixlip, and fields and trees and hedges started to be scattered between the new raw estates, did they begin to talk, and all their talk circled about the man they were going to bury, their mother's brother, their Uncle Peter McDermott.

He had been the only one in the family to stay behind with his parents on Gloria Bog where he'd been born. All the rest had scattered. Their Aunt Mary had died young in Walthamstow, London; Martin died in Milton, Massachusetts; Katie, the eldest, had died only the year before in Oneida, New York. With Peter's death they were all gone now, except their mother. She had been the last to leave the house. She first served her time in a shop in Carrick-on-Shannon and then moved to a greengrocer's-cum-confectioner's on the North Circular Road where she met their unreliable father, a traveller for Lemons Sweets.

While the powerful car slowed through Enfield they began to recall how their mother had taken them back to Gloria at the beginning of every summer, leaving their father to his own devices in the city. They spent every summer there on the bog from the end of June until early September. Their mother had always believed that only for the clean air of the bog and the plain wholesome food they would never have made it through the makeshifts of the city winter. Without the air and the plain food they'd never, never have got through, she used to proclaim like a thanksgiving.

As long as her own mother lived it was like a holiday to go there every summer – the toothless grandmother who sat all day in her rocking chair, her shoulders shawled, the grey hair drawn severely back into a bun, only rising to gather crumbs and potato skins into her black apron, and holding it like a great cloth bowl, she would shuffle out on to the street. She'd wait until all her brown hens had started to beat and clamour around her and then with a quick laugh she'd scatter everything that the apron held. Often before she came in she'd look across the wide acres of the bog, the stunted birch trees, the faint blue of the heather, the white puffs of bog cotton trembling in every wind to the green slopes of Killeelan and walled evergreens high on the hill and say, 'I suppose it won't be long till I'm with the rest of them there.'

'You shouldn't talk like that, Mother,' they remembered their mother's ritual scold.

'There's not much else to think about at my age. The gaps between the bog holes are not getting wider.'

One summer the brown rocking chair was empty. Peter lived alone in the house. Though their mother worked from morning to night in the house, tidying, cleaning, sewing, cooking, he made it clear that he didn't want her any more, but she ignored him. Her want was greater than his desire to be rid of them and his fear of going against the old pieties prevented him from turning them away.

The old ease of the grandmother's time had gone. He showed them no welcome when they came, spent as little time in the house as possible, the days working in the fields, visiting other houses at night where, as soon as he had eaten, he complained to everybody about the burden he had to put up with. He never troubled to hide his relief when the day finally came at the end of the summer for them to leave. In the quick way of children, the three boys picked up his resentment and suffered its constraint. He hardly ever looked at Fonsie in his wheelchair, and it was fear that never allowed Fonsie to take his eyes from the back of his uncle's head and broad shoulders. Whenever Philly or John took him sandwiches and the Powers bottle of tea kept warm in the sock to the bog or meadow, they always instinctively took a step or two back after handing him the oilcloth bag. Out of loneliness there were times when he tried to talk to them but the constraint had so solidified that all they were ever able to give back were childish echoes of his own awkward questions. He never once acknowledged the work their mother had done in the house which was the way she had – the only way she had – of paying for their stay in the house of her own childhood. The one time they saw him happy was whenever her exasperation broke and she scolded him: he would smile as if all the days he had spent alone with his mother had suddenly returned. Once she noticed that he enjoyed these scolds, and even set to actively provoke them at every small turn, she would go more doggedly still than was her usual wont.

'What really used to get her dander up was the way he used to lift up his trousers by the crotch before he sat down to the table,' Fonsie said as the car approached Longford, and the brothers all laughed in their different ways.

'He looked as if he was always afraid he'd sit on his balls,' Philly said. 'He'll not have to worry about that any more.'

'His worries are over,' John said.

'Then, after our father died and she got that job in the laundry, that was the first summer we didn't go. She was very strange that summer. She'd take your head off if you talked. We never went again.'

'Strange, going down like this after all that,' John said vaguely.

'I was trying to say that in the house. It makes no sense to me but this man and Mother wouldn't listen,' Fonsie said. 'They were down my throat before I could open my mouth.'

'We're here now anyhow,' Philly said as the car crossed the narrow bridge at Carrick and they could look down at the Shannon. They were coming into country that they knew. They had suffered here.

'God, I don't know how she came here summer after summer when she wasn't wanted,' John said as the speeding car left behind the last curve of sluggish water.

'Well, she wasn't exactly leaving the Garden of Eden,' Philly said.

'It's terrible when you're young to come into a place where you know you're not wanted,' John said. 'I used to feel we were eating poor Peter out of house and home every summer. When you're a child you feel those sorts of things badly even though nobody notices. I see it still in the faces of the children I teach.'

'After all that we're coming down to bury the fucker. That's what gets me,' Fonsie said.

'He's dead now and belongs with all the dead,' Philly said. 'He wasn't all bad. Once I helped him drive cattle into the fair of Boyle. It was dark when

17

we set out. I had to run alongside them in the fields behind the hedges until they got too worn out to want to leave the road. After we sold the cattle up on the Green he took me to the Rockingham Arms. He bought me lemonade and ginger snaps and lifted me up on the counter and said I was a great gosson to the whole bar even if I had the misfortune to be from Dublin.'

'You make me sick,' Fonsie said angrily. 'The man wasn't civilized. I always felt if he got a chance he'd have put me in a bag with a stone and thrown me in a bog hole like that black whippet.'

'That's exaggerating now. He never did and we're almost there,' John said as the car went past the church and scattered houses of Cootehall, where they had come to Mass on Sundays and bought flour and tea and sugar.

'Now, fasten your seat-belts,' Philly said humorously as he turned slowly into the bog road. To their surprise the deep potholes were gone. The road had been tarred, the unruly hedges of sally and hazel and briar cut back. Occasionally a straying briar clawed at the windscreen, the only hint of the old wildness. When the hedges gave way to the field of wild raspberry canes, Philly slowed the car to a crawl, and then stopped. Suddenly the bog looked like an ocean stretched in front of them, its miles of heather and pale sedge broken by the stunted birch trees, and high against the evening sun the dark evergreens stood out on the top of Killeelan Hill.

'He'll be buried there the day after tomorrow.'

The house hadn't changed, whitewashed, asbestos-roofed, the chestnut tree in front standing in the middle of the green fields on the edge of the bog; but the road was now tarred to the door, and all around the house new cattle sheds had sprung up.

Four cars were parked on the street and the door of the small house was open. A man shading his eyes with his hand came to the doorway as soon as the Mercedes came to a stop. It was Jim Cullen, the man who had telephoned the news of the death, smaller now and white-haired. He welcomed the three brothers in turn as he shook their hands. 'I'm sorry for your trouble. You were great to come all the way. I wouldn't have known any of you except for Fonsie. Your poor mother didn't manage to come?'

'She wasn't up to it,' Philly said. 'She hasn't left the house in years.'

As soon as they entered the room everybody stood up and came towards them and shook hands: 'I'm sorry for your trouble.' There were three old men besides Jim Cullen, neighbours of the dead man who had known them as children. Mrs Cullen was the older woman. A younger man about their own age was a son of the Cullens, Michael, whom they remembered as a child, but he had so grown and changed that his appearance was stranger to them than the old men.

'It's hard to think that Peter, God rest him, is gone. It's terrible,' Jim Cullen said as he led them into the bedroom.

The room was empty. A clock somewhere had not been stopped. He looked very old and still in the bed. They would not have known him. His hands were enormous on the white sheet, the beads a thin dark trickle through the locked fingers. A white line crossed the weathered forehead where he had worn a hat or a cap. The three brothers blessed themselves, and after a pause John and Philly touched the huge rough hands clasped together on the sheet. They were very cold. Fonsie did not touch the hands, turning the chair round towards the kitchen before his brothers left the side of the bed.

In the kitchen Fonsie and Philly drank whiskey. Mrs Cullen said it was no trouble at all to make John a cup of tea and there were platefuls of cut sandwiches on the table. Jim Cullen started to take up the story of Peter's death. He had told it many times already and would tell it many times again during the next days.

'Every evening before dark Peter would come out into that garden at the side. It can be seen plain from our front door. He was proud, proud of that garden though most of what it grew he gave away.'

'You couldn't have a better neighbour. If he saw

you coming looking for help he'd drop whatever he was doing and swear black and blue that he was doing nothing at all,' an old man said.

'It was lucky,' Jim Cullen resumed. "This woman here was thinking of closing up the day and went out to the door before turning the key, and saw Peter in the garden. She saw him stoop a few times to pull up a weed or straighten something and then he stood for a long time; suddenly he just seemed to keel over into the furrow. She didn't like to call and waited for him to get up and when he didn't she ran for me out the back. I called when I went into the garden. There was no sight or sound. He was hidden under the potato stalks. I had to pull them back before I was able to see anything. It was lucky she saw him fall. We'd have had to look all over the bog for days before we'd have ever thought of searching in the stalks.'

'Poor Peter was all right,' Philly said emotionally. 'I'll never forget the day he put me up on the counter of the Rockingham Arms.'

He was the only brother who seemed in any way

moved by the death. John looked cautiously from face to face but whatever he found in the faces did not move him to speak. Fonsie had finished the whiskey he'd been given on coming from the room and appeared to sit in his wheelchair in furious resentment. Then, one by one, as if in obedience to some hidden signal or law, everybody in the room rose and shook hands with the three brothers in turn and left them alone with Jim and Maggie Cullen.

As soon as the house had emptied Jim Cullen signalled that he wanted them to come down for a minute to the lower room, which had hardly been used or changed since they had slept there as children: the bed that sank in the centre, the plywood wardrobe, the blue paint of the windowsill half flaked away and the small window that looked out on all of Gloria, straight across to the dark trees of Killeelan. First, Jim showed them a bill for whiskey, beer, stout, bread, ham, tomatoes, butter, cheese, sherry, tea, milk, sugar. He read out the words slowly and with difficulty.

'I got it all in Henry's. Indeed, you saw it all out on the table. It wasn't much but I wasn't certain if anybody was coming down and of course I'd be glad to pay it myself for poor Peter. You'll probably want to get more. When word gets out that you're here there could be a flood of visitors before the end of the night.' He took from a coat a large worn bulging wallet. 'Peter, God rest him, was carrying this when he fell. I didn't count it but there seems to be more than a lock of hundreds in the wallet.'

Philly took the handwritten bill and the wallet.

'Would Peter not have made a will?' John asked.

'No. He'd not have made a will,' Jim Cullen replied.

'How can we be sure?'

'That was the kind of him. He'd think it unlucky. It's not right but people like Peter think they're going to live for ever. Now that the rest of them has gone, except your mother, everything that Peter has goes to yous,' Jim Cullen continued as if he had already given it considerable thought. 'I ordered the coffin and hearse from Beirne's in Boyle. I did not order the cheapest – Peter never behaved like a small man when he went out – but he wouldn't like to see too much money going down into the ground either. Now that you're all here you can change all that if you think it's not right.'

'Not one thing will be changed, Jim,' Philly said emotionally.

Then there's this key.' Jim Cullen held up a small key on a string. 'You'll find it opens the iron box in the press above in the bedroom. I didn't go near the box and I don't want to know what's in it. The key was around his poor neck when he fell. I'd do anything in the world for Peter.'

'You've done too much already. You've gone to far too much trouble,' Philly said.

'Far too much,' John echoed. 'We can't thank you enough.'

'I couldn't do less,' Jim Cullen replied. 'Poor Peter was one great neighbour. Anything you ever did for him he made sure you got back double.'

Fonsie alone did not say a word. He glowed in a private, silent resentment that shut out everything around him. His lips moved from time to time but they were speaking to some darkness seething within. It was relief to move out of the small cramped room. Mrs Cullen rose from the table as soon as they came from the room as if making herself ready to help in any way she could.

'Would you like to come with us to the village?' Philly asked.

'No, thanks,' Jim Cullen answered. 'I have a few hours' shuffling to do at home but then I'll be back.'

When it seemed as if the three brothers were going together to the village the Cullens looked from one to the other and Jim Cullen said, 'It'd be better if one of you stayed . . . in case of callers.'

John volunteered to stay. Philly had the car keys in his hand and Fonsie had already moved out to the car.

'I'll stay as well,' Mrs Cullen said. 'In case John might not know some of the callers.'

While Fonsie had been silent within the house, as soon as the car moved out of the open bog into that part of the lane enclosed by briars and small trees, an angry outpouring burst out like released water. Everything was gathered into the rushing complaint: the poor key with the string, keeling over in the potato stalks, the bloody wallet, the beads in the huge hands that he always felt wanted to choke him, the bit of cotton sticking out of the corner of the dead man's mouth. The whole thing was barbaric, uncivilized, obscene: they should never have come.

'Isn't it as good anyhow as having the whole thing swept under the carpet as it is in the city?' Philly argued reasonably.

'You mean we should bark ourselves because we don't keep a dog?'

'You make no effort,' Philly said. 'You never once opened your mouth in the house . . . In Dublin even when you're going to shop it takes you a half-hour to get from one end of a street to the next.'

'I never opened my mouth in the house and I never will. Through all those summers I never talked to anybody in the house but Mother and only when the house was empty. We were all made to feel that way – even Mother admitted that – but I was made to feel worse than useless. Every time I caught Peter looking at me I knew he was thinking that there was nothing wrong with me that a big stone and a rope and a deep bog hole couldn't solve.'

'You only thought that,' Philly said gently.

'Peter thought it too.'

'Well then, if he did – which I doubt – he thinks it no more.'

'By the way, you were very quick to pocket his wallet,' Fonsie said quickly as if changing the attack.

'That's because nobody else seemed ready to take it. But you take it if that's what you want.' Philly took the wallet from his pocket and offered it to Fonsie.

'I don't want it.' Fonsie refused the wallet roughly.

'We'd better look into it, then. We'll never get a quieter chance again in the next days.'

They were on a long straight stretch of road just outside the village. Philly moved the car in on to the grass margin. He left the engine running.

'There are thousands in this wallet,' Philly said simply after opening the wallet and fingering the notes.

'You'd think the fool would have put it in a bank where it'd be safe and earning interest.'

'Peter wouldn't put it in a bank. It might earn a tax inspector and a few awkward questions as well as interest,' Philly said as if he already was in possession of some of his dead uncle's knowledge and presence.

With the exception of the huge evergreens that used to shelter the church, the village had not changed at all. They had been cut down. Without the rich trees the church looked huge and plain and ugly in its nakedness.

'There's nothing more empty than a space you knew once when it was full,' Fonsie said.

'What do you mean?'

'Can you not see the trees?' Fonsie gestured irritably.

'The trees are gone.'

'That's what I mean. They were there and they're no longer there. Can you not see?'

Philly pressed Fonsie to come into the bar-grocery but he could not be persuaded. He said that he preferred to wait in the car. When Fonsie preferred something, with that kind of pointed politeness, Philly knew from old exasperations that it was useless to try to talk, and he left him there in silence.

'You must be one of the Ryans, then. You're welcome but I'm very sorry about poor Peter. You wouldn't be John, now? No? John stayed below in the house. You're Philly, then, and that's Fonsie out in the car. He won't come in? Your poor mother didn't come? I'm very sorry about Peter.' The old man with a limp behind the counter repeated each scrap of information after Philly as soon as it was given between his own hesitant questions and interjections.

'You must be Luke Henry, then?' Philly asked.

'The very man and still going strong. I remember you well coming in the summers. It must be at least ten years.'

'No. Twenty years now.'

'Twenty.' He shook his head. 'You'd never think. Terror how they go. It may be stiff pedalling for the first years but, I fear, after a bit, it is all freewheeling.' When Luke smiled his face became strangely boyish. 'What'll you have? On the house! A large brandy?'

'No, nothing at all. I just want to get a few things for the wake.'

'You'll have to have something, seeing what happened.'

'Just a pint, then. A pint of Guinness.'

'What will Fonsie have?'

'He's all right. He couldn't be got to come in out of the car. He's that bit upset,' Philly said.

'He'll have to have something,' Luke said doggedly.

'Well, a pint, then. I'll take it out to him myself. He's that bit upset.'

When Philly opened the door of the car and offered him Luke's pint, Fonsie said, 'What's this fucking thing for?'

'Nothing would do him but to send you out a

drink when I said you wouldn't come in.'

'What am I supposed to do with it?'

'Put it in your pocket. Use it for hair oil. It's about time you came off your high horse and took things the way they are offered.' Fonsie's aggression was suddenly met with equal aggression, and before he had time to counter, Philly closed the car door, leaving him alone with the pint in his hand.

Back inside the bar Philly raised his glass. 'Good luck. Thanks, Luke.'

'To the man that's gone,' Luke said. 'There was no sides to poor Peter. He was straight and thick. We could do with more like him.'

Philly drank quickly and then started his order: several bottles of whiskey, gin, vodka, sherry, brandy, stout, beer, lemonade, orange, and loaves, butter, tea, coffee, ham and breasts of turkey. Luke wrote down each item as it was called. Several times he tried to cut down the order – 'It's too much, too much' he kept muttering – then, slowly, one by one, all the time checking the list, he placed each item on the counter, checking it against the list once more before packing everything into several cardboard boxes.

Philly pulled out a wad of money.

'No,' Luke refused the money firmly. 'We'll settle it all out here later. You'll have lots to bring back. Not even the crowd down in the bog will be able to eat and drink that much.' He managed a smile in which malice almost equalled wistfulness.

After they'd filled the boot with boxes, they stacked more in the back seat and on one side of the folded wheelchair. Luke shook Fonsie's hand as he helped to carry out the boxes to the car. 'I'm sorry for your trouble'; but if Fonsie made any response it was inaudible. When they finished, Philly lifted the empty pint glass from the dashboard and handed it to Luke with a wink. Luke raised the pint glass in a sly gesture to indicate that he was more than well acquainted with the strange ways of the world.

'In all my life I never had to drink a pint sitting on my own in a car outside a public house. There's no manners round here. The people are savages,' Fonsie complained as soon as the car moved.

'You wouldn't come in and Luke meant only the best,' Philly said gruffly.

'Of course, as usual you had to go and make a five- or six-course meal out of the whole business.'

'What do you mean?'

'I thought you'd never stop coming out of the pub with the boxes. The boot is full. The back seat is jammed. You must have enough to start a bar-restaurant yourself.'

'They can be returned,' Philly said defensively. 'Luke wouldn't even take money. We wouldn't want to be disgraced by running out of drink in the middle of the wake. Luke said, everybody said, there was never anything small about Uncle Peter. He wouldn't want anything to run short at his wake. The McDermotts were always big people.'

'They were in their shite,' Fonsie said furiously. 'He made us feel we were stealing bread out of his mouth. But that's you all over. Big, big, big,' he taunted. 'That's why people in Dublin are fed up with you. You always have to make the big splash. You live in a rathole in the desert for eighteen months, then you come out and do the big fellow. People don't want that. They want to go about their own normal lives. They don't want your drinks or big blow.'

There are no things more cruel than truths about ourselves spoken to us by another that are perceived to be at least half true. Left unsaid and hidden we feel they can be changed or eradicated, in time. Philly gripped Fonsie's shoulder in a despairing warning that he'd heard enough. They turned into the bog road to the house.

'We live in no rathole in the desert,' Philly said quietly. 'There's no hotel in Dublin to match where we live, except there's no booze, and sometimes that's no bad thing either.'

'That still doesn't take anything away from what I said.' Fonsie would not relent.

Without any warning, suddenly, they were out of the screen of small trees into the open bog. A low red sun west of Killeelan was spilling over the sedge and dark heather. Long shadows stretched out from the small birches scattered all over the bog.

'What are you stopping for?' Fonsie demanded.

'Just looking at the bog. On evenings like this I used to think it was on fire. Other times the sedge looked like gold. I remember it well.'

'You're talking through your drainpipe,' Fonsie said as the car moved on. 'All I remember of these evenings is poor Mother hanging out the washing.'

'Wouldn't she hang it out in the morning?'

'She had too much to do in the morning. It shows how little you were about the house. She used to wash all of Peter's trousers. They never were washed from one year to the next. She used to say they were fit to walk around on their own. Often with a red sun there was the frost. She thought it freshened clothes.'

To their surprise there were already six cars on the street as they drew close to the house.

'News must have gone out already that you've bought the world of booze,' Fonsie said as they drew up in front of the door, and his humour was not improved by having to sit in the car while all the boxes in the boot were carried into the house before the wheelchair could be taken out.

John was getting on famously with the people in the house who had come while his two brothers had been away. In fact, he got on better with strangers than with either of his brothers. He was a good listener. At school he had been a brilliant student, winning scholarships with ease all the way to university; but as soon as he graduated he disappeared into teaching. He was still teaching the same subjects in the same school where he had started, and appeared to dislike his work intensely though he was considered one of the best teachers in the school. Like most of his students and fellow teachers he seemed to live and work for the moment when the buzzer would end the school day.

'I don't want to be bothered,' was a phrase he used whenever new theories or educational practices came up in the classroom. 'They can go and cause trouble with their new ideas elsewhere. I just want to be left in peace.'

Their mother complained that his wife ran his whole life – she had been a nurse before they married – but others were less certain. They felt he encouraged her innate bossiness so that he could the better shelter unbothered behind it like a deep hedge. When offered the headship of the school, he had turned it down without consulting his wife. She had been deeply hurt when she heard of the offer from the wife of another teacher. She would have loved to have gone to the supermarket and church as the headmaster's wife. Her dismay forced her to ask him if it was true. 'You should at least have told me.' His admission that he'd refused the promotion increased her hurt. 'I didn't want to bother you,' he said so finally that she was silenced.

When the two brothers came back to the house, he gradually moved back into a corner, listening with perfect attention to anybody who came to him, while before he had been energetically welcoming visitors, showing them to the corpse room, getting them drinks and putting them at ease. Once Philly and Fonsie came into the house he turned it all over to them. The new callers lined up in front of them to shake their hands in turn.

I'm sorry about poor Peter. I'm sorry for your trouble. Very sorry.'

'Thank you for coming. I know that. I know that well,' Philly answered equally ceremoniously, and his ready words covered Fonsie's stubborn silence.

Despite the aspersion Fonsie cast on the early mourners, very little was drunk or eaten that night. Maggie Cullen made sandwiches with the ham and turkey and tomatoes and sliced loaves. Her daughter-in-law cut the sandwiches into small squares and handed them around on a large oval plate with blue flowers around the rim. Tea was made in a big kettle. There were not many glasses in the house but few had to drink wine or whiskey from cups. Those that drank beer or stout refused all offers of cup or glass and drank from the bottles. Some who smoked had a curious, studious habit of dropping their cigarette butts carefully down the narrow necks of the bottles. Some held up the bottles like children to listen to the smouldering ash hiss in the beer dregs. By morning, butts could be seen floating in the bottoms of several of the bottles like trapped wasps.

All through the evening and night people kept coming to the house while others who had come earlier quietly left. First they shook hands with the three brothers, then went to the upper room, knelt by the bed; and when they rose they touched the dead hands or forehead in a gesture of leave-taking or communion, and then sat on one of the chairs by the bed. When new people came in to the room and knelt by the bed they left their chairs and returned to the front room where they were offered food and drink and joined in the free, unceasing talk and laughter. Almost all the talk was of the dead man. Much of it was in the form of stories. All of them showed the dead man winning out in life and the few times he had been forced to concede defeat it had been with stubbornness or wit. No surrender here, were his great words.

The only thing he ever regretted was never having learned to drive a car. 'We always told him we'd drive him anywhere he wanted to go,' Jim Cullen said. 'But he'd never ask. He was too proud, and when we'd take him to town on Saturdays we'd have to make it appear that we needed him along for company; then he'd want to buy you the world of drink. When the children were young he'd load them down with money or oranges and chocolates. Then, out of the blue, he said to me once that he might be dead if he'd ever learned to drive: he'd noticed that many who drove cars had died, while a lot of those who had to walk or cycle like himself were still battering around.'

From the top of the dresser a horse made from matchsticks and mounted on a rough board was taken down. The thin lines of the matchsticks were cunningly spliced and glued together to suggest the shape of a straining horse in the motion of plough-ing or mowing. A pig was found among the plates, several sheep that were subtly different from one another, as well as what looked like a tired old collie, all made from the same curved and spliced matchsticks.

'He was always looking for matches. Even in town on Saturdays you'd see him picking them up from the bar floor. He could do anything with them. The children loved the animals he'd give them. Seldom they broke them. Though our crowd are grown we still have several he made in the house. He never liked TV. That's what you'd find him at on any winter's night if you wandered in on your *ceilidh*. He could nearly make those matchsticks talk.'

It was as if the house had been sundered into two distinct and separate elements, and yet each reflected and measured the other as much as the earth and the sky. In the upper room there was silence, the people there keeping vigil by the body where it lay in the stillness and awe of the last change; while in the lower room that life was being resurrected with more vividness than it could ever have had in the long days and years it had been given.

Though all the clocks in the house had now been silenced everybody seemed to know at once when it was midnight and all the mourners knelt except Fonsie and two very old women. The two rooms were joined as the Rosary was recited but as soon as the prayers ended each room took on again its separate entity.

Fonsie signalled to Philly that he wanted to go outside. Philly knew immediately that his brother wanted to relieve himself. In the city he never allowed any help but here he was afraid of the emptiness and darkness of the night outside the house and the strange ground. It was a clear moonlit night without a murmur of wind, and the acres of pale sedge were all lit up, giving back much of the light it was receiving, so that the places that were covered with heather melted into a soft blackness and the scattered shadows of the small birches were soft and dark on the cold sedge. High up and far off they could hear an aeroplane and soon they picked it out by the pulsing of its white nightlight as it crossed their stretch of sky. The tall evergreens within the pale stone wall on the top of Killeelan were dark and gathered together against the moonlight. As if to give something back to his brother for accompanying him into the night, Fonsie said as he was relieving himself in the shadowed corner of the house, 'Mother remembers seeing the first car in this place. She says she was ten. All of them from the bog rushed out to the far road to see the car pass. It's strange to think of people living still who didn't grow up with cars.'

'Maybe they were as well off,' Philly said.

'How could they be as well off?'

'Would Peter in there now be better off?'

'I thought it was life we were talking about. If they were that well off why had they all to do their best to get to hell out of the place?'

'I was only thinking that a lot of life never changes. If the rich could get the poor to die for them the rich would never die,' Philly said belligerently. It didn't take much or long for an edge to come between them, but before it could grow they went back into the house. Not until close to daylight did the crowd of mourners start to thin.

During all this time John had been the most careful of the three brothers. He had drunk less than either of the other two, had stayed almost as silent as Fonsie, and now he noticed each person's departure and accompanied them out to their cars to thank them for coming to Peter's wake as if he had been doing it all his life. By the time the last car left, the moon was still in the sky but was well whitened by the rising sun. The sedge had lost its brightness and taken on the dull colour of wheat. All that was left in the house with the dead man and his three nephews were the Cullens and a local woman who had helped with tea and sandwiches through the night. By that time they had all acquired the heady, vaguely uplifting spiritual feeling that comes in the early stages of exhaustion and is often strikingly visible in the faces of the old or sick.

In the same vague, absent, dreamlike way, the day drifted towards evening. Whenever they came to the door they saw a light, freshening wind moving over the sedge as if it were passing over water. Odd callers continued coming to the house throughout the day, and after they spent time with the dead man in the room they were given food and drink and they sat and talked. Most of their talk was empty and tired by now and had none of the vigour of the night before. Mrs Cullen took great care to ensure that the upper room was never left empty, that someone was always there by Peter's side on this his last day in the house. Shortly after five the hearse arrived and the coffin was taken in. It was clear that Luke had been right and that most of the drink Philly had ordered would have to be returned. Immediately behind the hearse was a late, brief flurry of callers. Shortly before six the body was laid in the coffin and, with a perfunctory little swish of beads, the undertaker began the decade of the Rosary. The coffin was closed and taken out to the hearse. Many cars had taken up position on the narrow road to accompany the hearse to the church.

After they left the coffin before the high altar in the church, some of the mourners crossed the road to Luke's Bar. There, Philly bought everybody a round of drinks but when he attempted to buy a second round both Luke and Jim Cullen stopped him. Custom allowed one round but no more. Instead he ordered a pint of stout for himself and Fonsie, and John shook his head to the offer of a second drink. Then when Philly went to pay for the two drinks Luke pushed the money back to him and said that Jim Cullen had just paid.

People offered to put the brothers up for the night but Fonsie especially would not hear of staying in a strange house. He insisted on going to the hotel in town. As soon as they had drunk the second pint and said their goodbyes Philly drove John and Fonsie to the Royal Hotel. He waited until they were given rooms and then prepared to leave.

'Aren't you staying here?' Fonsie asked sharply when he saw that Philly was about to leave him alone with John.

'No.'

'Where are you putting your carcass?'

'Let that be no worry of yours,' Philly said coolly.

'I don't think a more awkward man ever was born. Even Mother agrees on that count.'

'I'll see you around nine in the morning,' Philly said to John as they made an appointment to see Reynolds, the solicitor, before the funeral Mass at eleven.

Philly noticed that both the young Cullens and the older couple had returned from the removal by the two cars parked outside their house. Peter's house was unlocked and eerily empty, everything in it exactly as it was when the coffin was taken out. On impulse he took three bottles of whiskey from one of the boxes stacked beneath the table and walked with the bottles over to Cullen's house. They'd seen him coming from the road and Jim Cullen went out to meet him before he reached the door.

'I'm afraid you caught us in the act,' Mrs Cullen laughed. The four of them had been sitting at the table, the two men drinking what looked like glasses of whiskey, the women cups of tea and biscuits.

'Another half-hour and you'd have found us in the nest,' Jim Cullen said. 'We didn't realize how tired we were until after we came in from looking at our own cattle and Peter's. We decided to have this last drink and then hit off. We'll miss Peter.'

Without asking him, Mrs Cullen poured him a glass of whiskey and a chair was pulled out for him at the table. Water was added to the whiskey from a glass jug. He placed the three bottles on the table. 'I just brought over these before everything goes back to the shop.'

'It's far too much,' they responded. 'We didn't want anything.'

'I know that but it's still too little.' He seemed to reach far back to his mother or uncle for the right thing to say. 'It's just a show of something for all that you've done.'

'Thanks but it's still far too much.' They all seemed to be pleased at once and took and put the three bottles away. They then offered him a bed but he said he'd manage well enough in their old room. 'I'm used to roughing it out there in the oil fields,' he lied; and not many minutes after that, seeing Mrs Cullen stifle a yawn, he drank down his whiskey and left. Jim Cullen accompanied him as far as the road and stood there until Philly had gone some distance towards his uncle's house before turning slowly back.

In the house Philly went from room to room to let in fresh air but found that all the windows were stuck. He left the doors to the rooms open and the front door open on the bog. In the lower room he placed an eiderdown on the old hollowed bed and in the upper room he drew the top sheet up over where the corpse had lain until it covered both the whole of the bed and pillow. He then took the iron box from the cupboard and unlocked it on the table in the front room. Before starting to go through the box he got a glass and half filled it with whiskey. He found very old deeds tied with legal ribbon as he drank, cattle cards, a large wad of notes in a rubber band, a number of scattered US dollar notes, a one-hundred-dollar bill, some shop receipts ready to fall apart, and a gold wedding ring. He put the parchment to one side to take to the solicitor the next morning. The notes he placed in a brown envelope before locking the box and placing it back in the cupboard. He poured another large whiskey. On a whim he went and took down some of the matchstick figures that they had looked at the night before – a few of the sheep, a little pig, the dray-horse and cart, a delicate greyhound on a board with its neck straining out from the bent knees like a snake's as if about to pick a turning rabbit or hare from the ground. He moved them here and there on the table with his finger as he drank when, putting his glass down, his arm leaned on the slender suggestion of a horse, which crumpled and fell apart. Almost covertly he gathered the remains of the figure, the cart and scattered matches, and put them in his pocket to dispose of later. Quickly and uneasily he restored the sheep and pig and hound to the safety of the shelf. Then he moved his chair out into the doorway and poured more whiskey.

He thought of Peter sitting alone here at night

making the shapes of animals out of matchsticks, of those same hands now in a coffin before the high altar of Cootehall church. Tomorrow he'd lie in the earth on the top of Killeelan Hill. A man is born. He dies. Where he himself stood now on the path between those two points could not be known. He felt as much like the child that came each summer years ago to this bog from the city as the rough unfinished man he knew himself to be in the eyes of others, but feelings had nothing to do with it. He must be already well out past halfway.

The moon of the night before lit the pale sedge. He could see the dark shapes of the heather, the light on the larger lakes of sedge, but he had no desire to walk out into the night. Blurred with tiredness and whiskey, all shapes and lives seemed to merge comfortably into one another as the pale, ghostly sedge and the dark heather merged under the moon. Except for the stirrings of animals about the house and a kittiwake calling sharply high up over the bog and the barking of distant dogs the night was completely silent. There was not even a

passing motor. But before he lay down like a dog
under the eiderdown in the lower room he remembered to set the alarm of his travelling clock for
seven the next morning.

In spite of a throbbing forehead he was the first
person in the dining-room of the Royal Hotel for
breakfast the next morning. After managing to
get through most of a big fry – sausages, black
pudding, bacon, scrambled eggs and three pots
of black coffee – he was beginning to feel much
better when Fonsie and John came in for their
breakfast.

I wouldn't advise the coffee though I'm awash
with the stuff,' Philly said as the two brothers
looked through the menu.

'We never have coffee in the house except when
you're back,' Fonsie said.

'I got used to it out there. The Americans drink
nothing else throughout the day.'

'They're welcome to it,' Fonsie said.

'John looked from one brother to the other but
kept his silence. Both brothers ordered tea and

scrambled eggs on toast.

'What did you two do last night?'

'I'm afraid we had pints, too many pints,' John answered.

'You had no pints, only glasses,' Fonsie said.

'It all totted up to pints and there were too many. This wild life doesn't suit me. How you are able to move around this morning I don't know.'

'That's nothing,' Fonsie said. 'And you should see yer man here when he gets going; then you'd have a chance to talk. It's all or nothing. There's never any turning back.'

As Philly was visibly discomforted, John asked, 'What did you do?'

'I thanked the Cullens.'

'More whiskey,' Fonsie crowed.

Then I opened the iron box,' Philly ignored the gibe. 'I found the deeds. We'll need them for the lawyer in a few minutes. And there was another wad of money. There was sterling and dollars and a few Australian notes as well.'

'The sterling and dollars came from the brother

and sister. They were probably sent to the mother and never cashed. God knows where the Australian came from,' John said.

'It all comes to thousands,' Philly said.

'When we used to go there you'd think we were starving him out of the place.'

'They probably didn't have it then.'

'Even if they did it would still have been the same. It's a way of thinking.'

'The poor fucker, it'd make you laugh,' Fonsie said. 'Making pigs and horses out of matchsticks in the night, slaving on the bog or running after cattle in the day, when he could have gone out and had himself a good time.'

'Maybe that was his way of having a good time,' John said carefully.

'It'll get some good scattering now,' Fonsie laughed at Philly.

'Are you sure?' Philly said sternly back. 'It all goes to Mother anyhow. She's the next of kin. Maybe you'll give it the scattering? I have lots for myself.'

'Mr Big again,' Fonsie jeered.

'It's time to go to see this lawyer. Do you want to come?'

'I have more sense,' Fonsie answered angrily.

The brown photos around the walls of the solicitor's waiting room as well as the heavy mahogany table and leather chairs told that the practice was old, that it had been passed from grandfather Reynolds to father to son. The son was about fifty, dressed in a beautifully cut dark pinstripe suit, his grey hair parted in the centre. His manner was soft and urbane and quietly watchful.

Philly had asked John to state their business, which he did with simple clarity. As he spoke Philly marvelled at his brother. Even if it meant saving his own life he'd never have been able to put the business so neatly without sidetracking or leaving something out.

'My advice would be to lose that money,' the solicitor said when he had finished. 'Strictly, I shouldn't be giving that advice but as far as I'm concerned I never heard anything about it.'

Both brothers nodded their understanding and gratitude.

'Almost certainly there's no will. I'd have it if there was. I acted for Peter in a few matters. There was a case of trespass and harassment by a neighbouring family called Whelan a few years back. None of it was Peter's fault. They were a bad lot and solved our little problem by emigrating *en masse* to the States. Peter's friend, Jim Cullen, bought their land.'

Philly remembered wild black-haired Marie Whelan who had challenged him to fight on the bog road during one of those last summers. John just nodded that he remembered the family.

'So everything should go to your mother as the only surviving next of kin. As she is a certain age it should be acted on quickly and I'll be glad to act as soon as I learn what it is your mother wants.' As he spoke he opened the deeds Philly gave John to hand over. 'Peter never even bothered to have the deeds changed into his name. The place is in your grandfather's name and this document was drawn up by my grandfather.'

'Would the place itself be worth much?' Philly's sudden blunt question surprised John. Out of his quietness Mr Reynolds looked up at him sharply.

'I fear not a great deal. Ten or eleven thousand. A little more if there was local competition. I'd say fourteen at the very most.'

'You can't buy a room for that in the city and there's almost thirty acres with the small house.'

'Well, it's not the city and I do not think Gloria Bog is ever likely to become the Costa Brava.'

Philly noticed that both the solicitor and his brother were looking at him with withdrawn suspicion if not distaste. They were plainly thinking that greed had propelled him to stumble into the inquiry he had made when it was the last thing in the world he had in mind. Before anything further could be said, the solicitor was shaking both their hands at the door and nodding over their shoulders to the receptionist behind her desk across the hallway to take their particulars before showing them out.

In contrast to the removal of the previous evening, when the church had been full to overflowing,

there were only a few dozen people at the funeral
Mass. Eight cars followed the hearse to Killeelan, and only the Mercedes turned into the narrow
laneway behind the hearse. The other mourners
abandoned their cars at the road and entered the
lane on foot. Blackthorn and briar scraped against
the windscreen and sides of the Mercedes as they
moved behind the hearse's slow pace. At the end
of the lane there was a small clearing in front of
the limestone wall that ringed the foot of Killeelan
Hill. There was just enough space in the clearing
for the hearse and the Mercedes to park on either
side of the small iron gate in the wall. The coffin was taken from the hearse and placed on the
shoulders of John and Philly and the two Cullens.
The gate was just wide enough for them to go
through. Fonsie alone stayed behind in the front
seat of the Mercedes and watched the coffin as it
slowly climbed the hill on the four shoulders. The
coffin went up and up the steep hill, sometimes
swaying dangerously, and then anxious hands of
the immediate followers would go up against the

back of the coffin. The shadows of the clouds swept continually over the green hill and brown varnish of the coffin. Away on the bog they were a darker, deeper shadow as the clouds travelled swiftly over the pale sedge. Three times the small snail-like cortege stopped completely for the bearers to be changed. As far as Fonsie could see – he would have needed binoculars to be certain – they were the original bearers, his brothers and the two Cullens, who took up the coffin the third and last time and carried it through the small gate in the wall around the graveyard on the hilltop. Then it was only the coffin itself and the heads of the mourners that could be seen until they were lost in the graveyard evergreens. In spite of his irritation at this useless ceremony, that seemed only to show some deep love of hardship or enslavement – they'd be hard put to situate the graveyard in a more difficult or inaccessible place except on the very top of a mountain – he found the coffin and the small band of toiling mourners unbearably moving as it made its low stumbling climb up the hill, and this deepened further his irritation and the sense of complete uselessness.

Suddenly he was startled by the noise of a car coming very fast up the narrow lane and braking to a stop behind the hearse. A priest in a long black soutane and white surplice with a purple stole over his shoulders got out of the car carrying a fat black breviary. Seeing Fonsie, he saluted briskly as he went through the open gate. Then, bent almost double, he started to climb quickly like an enormous black-and-white crab after the coffin. Watching him climb, Fonsie laughed harshly before starting to fiddle with the car radio.

After a long interval the priest was the first to come down the hill, accompanied by two middle-aged men, the most solid looking and conventional of the mourners. The priest carried his surplice and stole on his arm. The long black soutane looked strangely menacing between the two attentive men in suits as they came down. Fonsie reached over to turn off the rock and roll playing on the radio as they drew close, but, in a sudden reversal, he

turned it up louder still. The three men looked towards the loud music as they came through the gate
but did not salute or nod. They got into the priest's
car and, as there was no turning place between the
hearse and the Mercedes, it proceeded to back out
of the narrow lane. Then in straggles of twos and
threes, people started to come down the hill. The
two brothers and Jim Cullen were the last to come
down. As soon as Philly got into the Mercedes he
turned off the radio.

'You'd think you'd show a bit more respect.'

'The radio station didn't know about the funeral.'

'I'm not talking about the radio station,' Philly
said.

'That Jim Cullen is a nice man,' John said in order to steer the talk away from what he saw as an
imminent clash. 'He's intelligent as well as decent.
Peter was lucky in his neighbour.'

'The Cullens,' Philly said as if searching for a
phrase. 'You couldn't, you couldn't if you tried get
better people than the Cullens.'

They drove straight from Killeelan to the Royal

for lunch. Not many people came, just the Cullens among the close neighbours and a few far-out cousins of the dead man. Philly bought a round for everyone and when he found no takers to his offer of a second round he did not press.

'Our friend seems to be restraining himself for once,' Fonsie remarked sarcastically to John as they moved from the bar to the restaurant.

'He's taking his cue from Jim Cullen. Philly is all right,' John said. 'It's those months and months out in the oil fields and then the excitement of coming home with all that money. It has to have an effect. Wouldn't it be worse if he got fond of the money?'

'It's still too much. It's not awanting,' Fonsie continued doggedly through a blurred recognition of all that Philly had given to their mother and to the small house over the years, and it caused him to stir uncomfortably.

The set meal was simple and good: hot vegetable soup, lamb chops with turnip and roast potatoes and peas, apple tart and cream, tea or coffee. While they were eating, the three gravediggers came into the dining-room and were given a separate table by one of the river windows. Philly got up as soon as they arrived to ensure that drinks were brought to their table.

When the meal ended, the three brothers drove back behind the Cullens' car to Gloria Bog. There they put all that was left of the booze back into the car. The Cullens accepted what food was left over but wouldn't hear of taking any more of the drink. 'We're not planning on holding another wake for a long time yet,' they said half humorously, half sadly. John helped with the boxes, Fonsie did not leave the car. As soon as Philly gave Jim Cullen the keys to the house John shook his hand and got back into the car with Fonsie and the boxes of booze, but still Philly continued talking to Jim Cullen outside the open house. In the rear mirror they saw Philly thrust a fistful of notes towards Jim Cullen. They noticed how large the old farmer's hands were as they gripped Philly by the wrist and pushed the hand and notes down into his jacket pocket, refusing stubbornly to accept any money. When John took his eyes from the mirror and the small sharp struggle between the two men, what met his eyes across the waste of pale sedge and heather was the rich dark waiting evergreens inside the back wall of Killeelan where they had buried Peter beside his father and mother only a few hours before. The colour of laughter is black. How dark is the end of all of life. Yet others carried the burden in the bright day on the hill. His shoulders shuddered slightly in revulsion and he wished himself back in the semi-detached suburbs with rosebeds outside in the garden.

'I thought you'd never finish,' Fonsie accused Philly when the big car began to move slowly out the bog road.

'There was things to be tidied up,' Philly said absently. 'Jim is going to take care of the place till I get back,' and as Fonsie was about to answer he found John's hands pressing his shoulders from the back seat in a plea not to speak. When they parked beside the door of the bar there was just place enough for another car to pass inside the church wall.

'Not that a car is likely to pass,' Philly joked as he and John carried the boxes in. When they had placed all of them on the counter they saw Luke reach for a brandy bottle on the high shelf.

'No, Luke,' Philly said. 'I'll have a pint if that's what you have in mind.'

'John'll have a pint, then, too.'

'I don't know,' John said in alarm. 'I haven't drunk as much in my life as the last few days. I feel poisoned.'

'Still, we're unlikely to have a day like this ever again,' Philly said as Luke pulled three pints.

'I don't think I'd survive many more such days,' John said.

'Wouldn't it be better to bring Fonsie in than to have him drinking out there in the car? It'll take me a while to make up all this. One thing I will say,' he said as he started to count the returned bottles. 'There was no danger of anybody running dry at Peter's wake.'

Fonsie protested when Philly went out to the car. It was too much trouble to get the wheelchair out of the boot. He didn't need drink. 'I'll take you in.' Philly offered his stooped neck and carried Fonsie into the bar like a child as he'd done many times when they were young and later when they were on certain sprees. He set him down in an armchair in front of the empty fireplace and brought his pint from the counter. It took Luke a long time to make up the bill, and when he eventually presented it to Philly, after many extra countings and checkings, he was full of apologies at what it had all come to.

'It'd be twice as much in the city,' Philly said energetically as he paid.

'I suppose it'd be as much anyhow,' Luke grumbled happily with relief and then at once started to draw another round of drinks which he insisted they take.

'It's on the house. It's not every day or year brings you down.'

Fonsie and Philly drank the second pint easily. John was already fuddled and unhappy and he drank reluctantly.

'I won't say goodbye.' Luke accompanied them

out to the car when they left. 'You'll have to be down again before long.'

'It'll not be long till we're down,' Philly answered firmly for all of them.

In Longford and Mullingar and Enfield Philly stopped on their way back to Dublin. John complained each time, but it was Philly who had command of the car. Each time he carried Fonsie into the bars – and in all of them the two drank pints – John refused to have anything in Mullingar or Longford but took a reluctant glass in Enfield.

'What'll you do if you have an accident and get breathalysed?'

'I'll not have an accident. And they can send the summons all the way out to the Saudis if I do.'

He drove fast but steadily into the city. He was silent as he drove. Increasingly, he seemed charged with an energy that was focused elsewhere and had been fuelled by every stop they had made. In the heart of the city, seeing a vacant place in front of Mulligan's where he had drunk on his own in the deep silence of the bar a few short mornings before, he pulled across the traffic and parked. Cars stopped to blow hard at him but he paid no attention as he parked and got out.

'We'll have a last drink here in the name of God before we face back to the mother,' Philly said as he carried Fonsie into the bar. There were now a few dozen early evening drinkers in the bar. Some of them seemed to know the brothers, but not well. John offered to move Fonsie from the table to an armchair but Fonsie said he preferred to remain where he was. John complained that he hadn't asked for the pint when the drinks were brought to the table.

'Is it a short you want, then?'

'No. I have had more drink today than I've had in years. I want nothing.'

'Don't drink it, then, if you don't want,' he was told roughly.

'Well, Peter, God rest him, was given a great send-off,' Philly said with deep satisfaction as he drank. 'I thank God I was back. I wouldn't have been away for the world. The church was packed for the removal. Every neighbour around was at Killeelan.'

'What else have they to do down there? It's the one excuse they have to get out of their houses,' Fonsie said.

'They honour the dead. That's what they do. People still mean something down there. They showed the respect they had for Peter.'

'Respect, my arse. Everybody is respected for a few days after they conk it because they don't have to be lived with any more. Oh, it's easy to honour the dead. It doesn't cost anything and gives them the chance to get out of their bloody houses before they start to eat one another within.'

An old argument started up, an argument they had had many times before without resolving anything, the strength of their difference betraying the hidden closeness.

Philly and Fonsie drained their glasses as John took the first sip from his pint and he looked uneasily from one to the other.

'You have it all crooked,' Philly said as he rose

to get more drink from the counter. John covered his glass with his palm to indicate that he wanted nothing more. When Philly came back with the two pints he started to speak before he had even put the glasses down on the table: he had all the blind dominating passion of someone in thrall to a single idea.

'I'll never forget it all the days of my life, the people coming to the house all through the night. The rows and rows of people at the removal passing by us in the front seat of the church grasping our hands. Coming in that small lane behind the hearse; then carrying Peter up that hill.'

Fonsie tried to speak but Philly raised his glass into his face and refused to be silenced.

'I felt something I never felt when we left the coffin on the edge of the grave. A rabbit hopped out of the briars a few yards off. He sat there and looked at us as if he didn't know what was going on before he bolted off. You could see the bog and all the shut houses next to Peter's below us. There wasn't even a wisp of smoke coming from any of the houses.

Everybody gathered around, and the priest started to speak of the dead and the Mystery and the Resurrection.'

'He's paid to do that and he was nearly late. I saw it all from the car,' Fonsie asserted. 'It was no mystery from the car. Several times I thought you were going to drop the coffin. It was more like a crowd of apes staggering up a hill with something they had just looted. The whole lot of you could have come right out of the Dark Ages, without even a dab of make-up. I thought a standard of living had replaced the struggle for survival ages ago.'

'I have to say I found the whole ceremony moving, but once is more than enough to go through that experience,' John said carefully. 'I think of Peter making those small animals out of matchsticks in the long nights on the bog. Some people pay money for that kind of work. Peter just did it out of some need.'

Philly either didn't hear or ignored what John said.

'It's a godsend they don't let you out often,' Fonsie said. 'People that exhibit in museums are a different kettle. Peter was just killing the nights on the bloody bog.'

'I'll never forget the boredom of those summers, watching Peter foot turf, making grabs at the butterflies that tossed about over the sedge. Once you closed your hand they always escaped,' John said as if something long buried in him was drawn out. 'I think he was making things out of matchsticks even then but we hardly noticed.'

'Peter never wanted us. Mother just forced us on him. He wasn't able to turn us away,' Fonsie said, the talk growing more and more rambling and at odds.

'He didn't turn us away, whether he wanted to or not,' Philly asserted truculently. 'I heard Mother say time and time again that we'd never have got through some of the winters but for those long summers on the bog.'

'She'd have to say that since she took us there.'

'It's over now. With Peter it's all finished. One of

the things that made the last days bearable for me was that everything we were doing was being done for the last time,' John said with such uncharacteristic volubility that the two brothers just stared.

'I'll say amen to that,' Fonsie said.

'It's far from over but we better have a last round for the road first.' Philly drained his glass and rose, and again John covered his three-quarter-full glass with his palm. 'As far as I can make out nothing is ever over.'

'Those two are tanks for drink, but they don't seem to have been pulling lately,' a drinker at the counter remarked to his companion as Philly passed by shakily with the pair of pints. 'The pale one not drinking looks like a brother as well. There must have been a family do.'

'You'd wonder where that wheelchair brother puts all that drink,' the other changed.

'He puts it where we all put it. You don't need legs, for God's sake, to take drink. Drink only gets down as far as your flute.'

'Gloria is far from over,' Philly said as he put the

two pints down on the table. 'Nothing is ever over. I'm going to take up in Peter's place.'

'You can't be that drunk,' Fonsie said dismissively.

'I'm not sober but I was never more certain of anything in my born life.'

'Didn't the lawyer say it'd go to Mother? What'll she do but sell?'

'I'm not sure she'll want to sell. She grew up there. It was in her family for generations.'

'I'm sure. I can tell you that now.'

'Well, it's even simpler, then. I'll buy the place off Mother,' Philly announced so decisively that Fonsie found himself looking at John.

'I'm out of this,' John said. 'What people do is their own business. All I ask is to be let go about my own life.'

'I've enough money to buy the place. You heard what the lawyer said it was worth. I'll give Mother its price and she can do with it what she likes.'

'We're sick these several years hearing about all you can buy,' Fonsie said angrily.

'Well, I'll go where people will not be sick, where there'll be no upcasting,' Philly said equally heatedly.

'What'll you do there?' John asked out of a desire to calm the heated talk.

'He'll grow onions.' Fonsie shook with laughter.

'I can't be going out to the oil fields for ever. It'll be a place to come home to. You saw how the little iron cross in the circle over the grave was eaten with rust. I'm going to have marble put up. Jim Cullen is going to look after Peter's cattle till I get back in six months and everything will be settled then.'

'You might even get married there,' Fonsie said sarcastically.

'It's unlikely but stranger things have happened, and I'll definitely be buried there. Mother will want to be buried there some day.'

'She'll be buried with our father out in Glasnevin.'

'I doubt that. Even the fish go back to where they came from. I'd say she's had more than enough of our poor father in one life to be going on with.

John here has a family, but it's about time you gave where you're going yourself some thought,' Philly spoke directly to Fonsie.

'If I were to go I'd want to go where there was people and a bit of life about, not on some God-forsaken hill out in the bog with a crow or a sheep or a bloody rabbit.'

'There's no *if* in this business, it's just *when.* I'm sorry to have to say it, but it betrays a great lack of maturity on your part,' Philly said with drunken severity.

'You can plant maturity out there in the bog, for all I care, and may it grow into an ornament.'

'We better be going,' John said.

Philly rose and took Fonsie into his arms. In spite of his unsteadiness he carried him easily out to the car. Fonsie was close to tears. He had always thought he could never lose Philly. The burly block of exasperation would always come and go from the oil fields. Now he would go out to bloody Gloria Bog instead. As he was put in the car, his tears turned to rage.

'Yes, you'll be a big shot down there at last,' he said. They'll be made up. They'll be getting a Christmas present. They'll be getting one great big lump of a Christmas present.'

'Look,' John said soothingly. 'Mother will be waiting. She'll want to hear everything. And I have another home I have to go to yet.'

'I followed it all on the clock,' the mother said. 'I knew the Mass for Peter was starting at eleven and I put the big alarm clock on the table. At twenty past twelve I could see the coffin going through the cattle gate at the foot of Killeelan.'

'They were like a crowd of apes carrying the coffin up the hill. I could see it all from the car. Several times they had to put up hands as if the coffin was going to fall off the shoulders and roll back down the hill.'

'Once it did fall off. Old Johnny Whelan's coffin rolled halfway down the hill and broke open. They had to tie the boards together with the ropes they use for lowering into the grave. Some said the Whelans were drunk, others said they were too weak with hunger to carry the coffin. The Whelans were never liked. They are all in America now.'

'Anyhow, we buried poor Peter,' Philly said, as if it was at last a fact.